The Tiniest Vampire

(and other silly things)

Matthew,
Thanks for
the
support!

written & illustrated
by
Jason L. Witter

The Tiniest Vampire (and other silly things)

ISBN-13: 978-1468055979
ISBN-10: 1468055976

First Edition: February 2016

www.facebook.com/witterworks
witterworks1@gmail.com

For
Leonard & Jane Witter,
my folks,
for they're
always there
for me.

Huge thanks to all the
Kickstarter Producer level backers!!!

Executive Producer

Ryan Denmark

Producers

Benjamin Nichols
Bruce Wong
David Valdez
Doug Montoya
Gregory Wong
Jay Lewis
Jess Jones
Kristin Berg
Brian & Kay Cunnane
Lupe H. Preciado
Matthew Lawrence Urbaniak

Mark Chavez
Nick Ganjei
Pumpkin
Radha Denmark
Shenoah Allen
Simon Platt
Suguru Oikawa
Winston Kou

Special thanks to Leonard & Jane Witter,
Scott Bryan, Jess Jones, Rob Buco,
Erin K. Moots, Jenn Daugherty, Phil Hughes
& Cardboard Playhouse Theatre Company.

Contents

Part 1: Small Poems

OPEN WITH EXTREME CAUTION!

Part 2: Medium Poems

Part 3: Large Poems

Small
Poems

The Tiniest Vampire

The tiniest vampire
lives in your shoe.
How he got there,
I haven't a clue.
But you needn't be fearful,
so long as you know,
to always be careful...
and keep an eye on your toe!
('cause he might bite it.)

12.

Watch Your Step

When Big Foot
came to town,
he wanted
to trick or treat.
The only problem was
he crushed
everybody
with his feet!
This would
have been okay,
a good time
could still be had,
if only
his big ol' feet
didn't smell
so big ol' bad!

Best Friends

Even

though

he's very different from me.

Even

though

we're a strange sight to see.

Even

though

no one else comprehends.

We've

become

the very best friends.

(As long as he's had somebody to eat

before we hang out.)

14.

16.

Oops

The mighty magician did surmise,
that he'd pull a rabbit
from the hat on his head.
Oh, what a surprise,
what a surprise!
When he pulled out
a cave troll instead!!!

Goblin Treats

There's a goblin in that house

who's really pretty vicious.

He thinks the taste of children

is down right quite delicious.

And he has a feeling

he'll be doing some good eating.

For soon will be the night

for all that trick or treating!

19.

Prince Charming's Plight

Cinderella don't need no fella.

Snow White is doing quite all right.

Jasmine's out living her own dreams.

Sleeping Beauty's growing coffee beans.

Ariel is happy living in the sea.

Elsa and Anna are just as chill as can be.

Tiana prefers books over frogs.

Belle has ditched the beast to rescue dogs.

Rapunzel's hair studio is oh so cool.

Pocahontas just got into law school.

Merida is busy being the bravest girl.

And Mulan wants

to save the whole darn world.

All of this is making

ol' Prince Charming quite irate,

'cause he's having a really hard time...

... finding himself a date!

Hump Day

The Hunchback of Notre Dame

likes to go out on a limb

and say that every Wednesday

is nicknamed just for him.

The middle of the week

makes him laugh and play

and puts a smile on his face

because it's hump day!

All right!

First Leaf

The first
leaf of fall
fell lonely from the tree.
With no one else around,
she did not know how to be.
She cried and
she cried
until
she
rea-
lized
that
at
long
last
she
was
finally free.

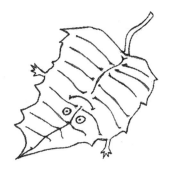

Tater Man

Tater Man, Tater Man,

does whatever a tater can.

Tater goo, tater poo,

what exactly does a tater do?

Not much.

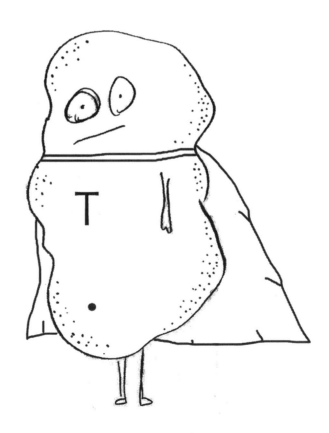

Eye Patch

Our goal was to find
the best pumpkin patch in the world,
and carve scary Jack-o-lanterns,
for all of the boys and the girls.
We searched, and we searched,
'til night and darkness did fall,
when finally we found it,
the greatest patch of them all.
But imagine our terror
when we lit up a match,
and saw nary a pumpkin,
because we were in an eye patch!!!

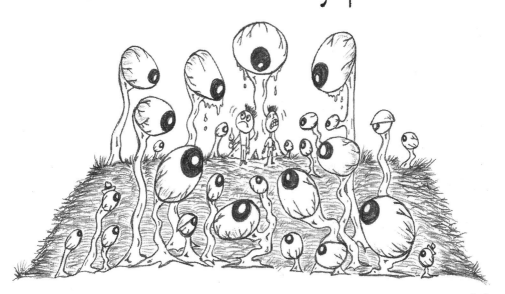

Ghouls Gone Wild

When little Iggy Imp
saw what day was here,
he threw his claws up high
and howled without a care!
He danced around the graves.
He giggled and he smiled.
Now 'twas finally time
for all the ghouls to go wild!
He ran through the streets.
He yelled and he screamed,
calling out to everyone:
Happy, happy, happy, happy,
HAPPY
HALLOWEEN!!!

28.

Medusa's Dilemma

Instead of hair on her head,
Medusa has snakes on her dome.
If you look at her face,
you turn right into stone.

Can she change her hairstyle?
The answer now is never,
for every barber that she meets,
turns into a statue forever!

Creature's Wish

The creature
from the black lagoon
wishes he was the creature
from sunny Cancun.
Then he would not feel
like such a buffoon.
He could hang out with his pal
Bobby Baboon,
Eat a fine dinner with his gal
Rosie Raccoon,
Drink some cream soda
at an old-fashioned saloon,
Travel around the world
in a hot air balloon,
Spend the morning watching
his favorite cartoon,
And maybe people
would stop trying to hit him...

...WITH AN EIGHT FOOT HARPOON!!!

31.

Drac & Frank's Tiny Adventure

Dracula and Frankenstein
decided one afternoon
to go to the Monster Fair
and each buy a balloon.
They went on some rides,
played games for a bit,
ate some funnel cake,
and that's really about it.
A rather uneventful day,
but they had a nice time.

Moment Monsters

The moment monsters

come and go

according to no plan.

So, when they do

decide to show,

be sure to hug them

while you can.

35.

All Dressed Up
and
Nowhere
To Go

Slender Man
has a problem.
No matter
how hard he tries,
wherever
he shows up,
people start to
drop like flies.
So, he's feeling
kind of bad,
he's feeling
kind of slighted,
'cause when
there's
a birthday
party...

... he never
gets invited.

Vampire Beach Party

A vampire at the beach
used to just be a lovely dream.
Now this goal can be reached,
when they use their sun SCREAM.
The vampire daddy,
and the vampire mommy,
can enjoy the sweet waves,
with their wicked son, Tommy.
They can play in the sand,
and go surfing and such,
and not have to worry...

... about turning to dust!

Excuse Me, Waiter: Part 1

There's a finger in my stew,
oh, a finger in my stew!
How it got there,
I haven't got a clue!
I thought it was a carrot,
oh, I thought it was a carrot!
But now I don't want
to even go near it!
I'd like to eat, you see,
oh, I'd like to eat, you see?
But it's kind of hard to eat
when my dinner keeps
pointing at me!!!

Excuse Me, Waiter: Part 2

There's a toe in my soup,
oh, a toe in my soup!
Why in the world
is there a toe in my soup?
There's a toe in my soup,
oh, a toe in my soup!
Well, I guess it's better
than a big ol' pile of poop!

The Knight in the Night

The knight in the night
perceived a perilous plight.
He could not see, you see,
so he stepped into the sea...
much to the hungry shark's delight!

43.

Stuck

The swamp monster awoke
with great plans for the day.
But when he got stuck in the toilet,
they were all flushed away.

Witch Stew

Eye of newt and toe of frog,
hair of bat and spit of dog,
leg of lizard and whisker of cat,
a little of this and a whole lot of that.
The witches are almost done
cooking up their stew,
too bad the last ingredient they need...
... is YOU!!!

Bubble Gum Girl

Little Polly Sue
blew the biggest bubbles.
She chewed gum in school,
and always was in trouble.
She blew a bubble so big,
it took her to the stars,
but when it finally popped,
she landed right on Mars.
Now that's where she lives,
and she thinks it's pretty dumb,
'cause Mars ain't got no stores...

...that sell chewing gum.

Lost

Oh my! There's a spaceship in the sky!

Oh dear! It's landing over there!

Oh wow! The door is open now!

Oh shoot! Maybe they'll be cute!

Oh blimey! Their skin's so green and slimy!

Oh dread! They have humungous heads!

Oh surprise! With great, big scary eyes!

Oh poo! What are we gonna do!

Oh snap! They're going to attack!

Oh man! The end is now at hand!

Oh run! Our days on Earth are done!

Oh, oh, oh, oh!

Oh... correction...

...they're just asking for directions.

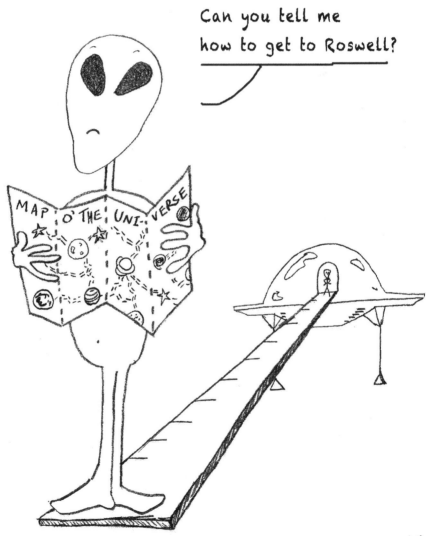

The Wolf Man's Big Night

The Wolf Man had a date,

so he wanted to look great.

But when he shaved his beard,

he just looked kind of weird.

The Invisible Man's Poem

Mummy Sniffles

The mummy ain't no dummy,

for when his nose gets runny,

he takes some tape

from off his tummy,

and wipes away the snot

and any other rot

whether anyone

really likes it or not!

Five Monsters

Five monsters sit atop an old wall.

They were out all night having a ball.

Now they are hungry for humans and flesh.

It'd be so nice to eat a body that's fresh.

But one monster said he'd given up meat.

Vegetables and fruit were all he would eat.

The others wondered what's wrong with his head,

but they quickly decided to just eat him instead.

Four monsters sit atop an old wall...

Night of the Living Dinner

When we came home
to eat last night,
we encountered
the strangest sight.
Our meal was not
on the table there,
'cause it had stood up
and taken the silverware.
We gulped and we screamed,
"this evening's a bust,"
for tonight is the night...

... our dinner eats us!

The Game Is Afoot

The zombies all wanted

To play a game of football.

But they had eaten all the players,

The referees and them all.

They devoured the gear,

The bags for the gym,

The shoulder pads and the gloves,

Even the good ol' pigskin.

All that remained,

A few helmets and shoes,

This posed a problem,

What's a zombie to do?

There would be no game of football,

But it didn't matter.

Because they soon decided...

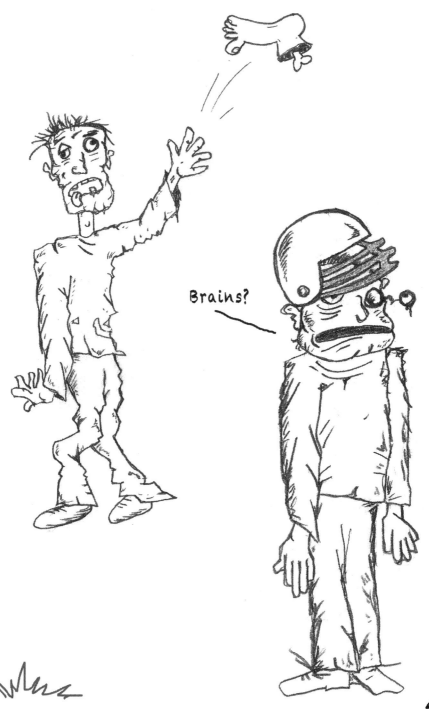

Werewolf Droppings

There's a werewolf
in the cupboard.
He used to live
under the sink.
But he pooped there
so much,
it really started
to stink.

He tried to blame the children,
but we knew they had been framed.
Now he hides in the pantry,
feeling lonely and ashamed.
So, here is the lesson,
if you want to save face,
when it comes to poopin',
make sure you go
in the right place!

The
Headless Snowman

The children ran out
of powder
before finishing
the snowman's head.
They thought about it
for an hour,
then made
a pumpkin face instead.
Now this fellow
is completed,
but only for
a day or so,
'cause once the sun
gets heated,
he'll lose
his whole torso!
(and then he'll be the
body-less pumpkin man.)

The Grumps

When you're in a bad mood
and feeling kind of bitter,
you're being paid a visit
by these naughty critters.
They make you so angry,
leaving you down in the dumps,
everything seems so stupid,
all your friends look like chumps.
There's a name for this malady,
but it's not the measles or the mumps.
No, my friend, I'm sorry to say,
you've got yourself this day
a really bad case of The Grumps.

Ol' Stumble Bottom

Here's a guy who's kind of neat.

You see, he rumbles,

And he skips,

And he mumbles,

And does the splits,

Solves Crossword jumbles,

And eats a chip,

With tasty crumbles,

Of blue cheese dip.

And he's humble,

And he's hip,

And does not grumble

About leaving a 20 percent tip.

Sometimes he stumbles,

And he slips,

And he tumbles,

And he trips,

And he fumbles,

And he flips...

...but he always lands on his feet.

Ta da.

Bobble and Gobble

There were two friends
named Bobble and Gobble.
They wanted an adventure,
so they hobbled and wobbled.
They had no bicycle.
They had no car.
And without any legs,
they did not get very far.
After hours and hours
of travelling so rough,
they moved only an inch,
but that was enough.
They stopped for a rest,
both feeling so tired.
Their whole bodies ached.
Their lungs were on fire.

Finally catching their breath,
they put their hands
to their hips,
and both solemnly agreed
to NEVER EVER
take any more trips!

Fast Guy

The fast guy
ran fast,
faster than
the fine wind.
But he ran

so

darn fast...
he left
his clothes
right
behind him!

Little Guy

Here's this little guy.

I cannot

think of a poem

for him.

No matter how hard I try.

(And, between you and me,

I think he's getting

kind of grumpy about it).

The Big Fat Kitty Cat

The big fat kitty cat

   sat with his hat.

The big fat kitty cat

   liked it like that.

   The End.

Cosmic Noodles

A creature came
from outer space
to wreak havoc on us,
the poor human race.
The damage he'd cause
would be
oodles
and oodles,
if only
his arms
and legs
were not
made out
of noodles!

errrr...

A Cookie for Krampus

Poor ol' Krampus
is getting a bad rap
for eating naughty children
who have done this and that.
We wonder, "why is he so grumpy
this happy holidy season?"
But if we stop to think,
we might just find the reason.
We'd put our hands to our hips
and smile and say, "oh, looky"
if someone
had just
thought
to leave
HIM
some milk
and a cookie!

for me?

73.

Medium
Poems

Big-Bellied Ghost

The Fitz family of Phoenix
is always troubled the most,
because they are haunted
by a big-bellied ghost.
Some ghosts are the meanest,
some ghosts are the maddest,
but the Fitz family ghost,
well, he's just the fattest!

Mom used to buy cookies,
she used to buy crackers,
but the ghost ate it all,
driving the whole family quackers.
Ice cream and cake,
and meat from some beast,
this specter ate it all
in a paranormal feast!

The ghost ate the turkey,
he ate the beef jerky,
he even ate the green chili
from old Albuquerque.
Whatever they had,
this ghost, he would eat it.
The Fitz Family feared
that they were defeated.

They would die of hunger,
the farm would be bought,
but then ol' Granny Fitz
had herself a thought.

She went to the store,
she bought carrots and beans,
broccoli and cauliflower,
two pounds of collared greens,
egg plants and spinach
snow peas and kale,
even some parsley,
'cause they were having a sale!

She brought the bag home,
set it down by the phone,
the fat ghost flew in
and let out a deep moan.
He cried and he cried,
and though they were edible,
the ghost just did not like
the taste of any vegetable!

Granny Fitz made a deal,
the ghost said he would try it.
He could still have a snack,
if he went on a diet.

So, while we've reached
the end of this ballad,
the Fitz Family of Phoenix...
and their ghost...
enjoy a nice Caesar salad!

Outside My Door

There's something outside my door...
Something hatching, something pawing,
something scratching, something clawing,
something sore, something dreadful,
goo and gore, it's got a headful,
something slimy, something scary,
something grimy, something hairy,
something gross, worse than a ghost,
blue ribbons at ugly shows,
it's won the most!
Something so awful
and terrible
and out-of-control
hideous,
it's impossible to stay calm!!!!!!

Oh... it's your mom.

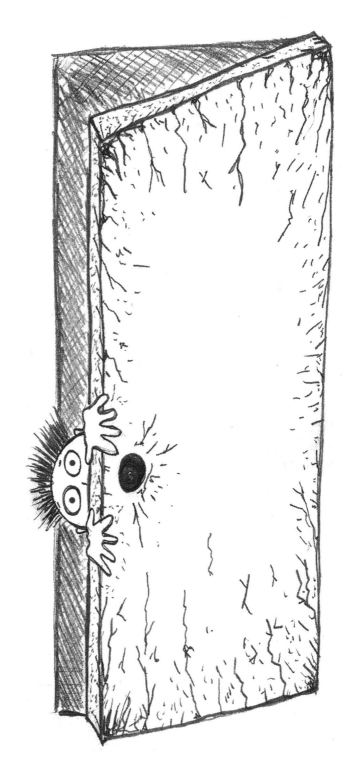

83.

13 Teeth

I got 13 teeth sitting in my mouth.
I use 'em to eat things
that I find around the house.
This one's for a hot dog
covered in mustard,
This one's for a bowl
of good vanilla custard,
This one's for a cheese
and chive tater chip,
This one's for a scoop
of guacamole dip,
This one's for a juicy
Thanksgiving turkey,
This one's for green chili
from old Albuquerque,
This one's for sour cream
and two nice potatoes,
This one's for three
sun dried up tomatoes,
This one's for the peaches
hanging in the trees,
This one's for a hunk of
stinky Limburger cheese,
This one's for a tasty
chocolate bar, if you please...

AND THIS ONE'S FOR EATING

NAUGHTY LITTLE CHILDREN

WHO DISOBEY THEIR PARENTS!!!!!!!!!!

Just kidding,
it's for eating carrots.

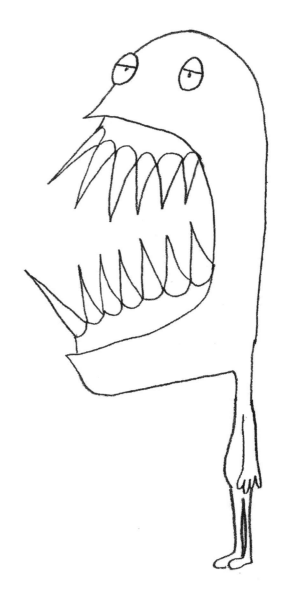

When a Witch Waits

If midnight is the witching hour,
when witches come out to play,
what are all those witches doing
with the rest of their whole day?

Do they pass the time
with boring, little chores?
Like using their old brooms
to sweep up all the floors?

Do they take off their hats,
and remove their black cloaks?
Put on sweaters and slacks
like every day folks?

Do they kick back,
watch the news and some sports?
And rub soothing cream
on all of their warts?

Do they have jobs
with bosses that yell?
Working nine to five,
and not casting spells?

Do they stare at the clock,
counting the hours?
Waiting for that time
when they can use all their powers?

I wonder if witches
lead rather dull lives,
until the clock strikes twelve
and announces midnight.

The Mendenhall Mice

The Mendenhall Mice
like to roll dice.
With every advance,
they take a chance.

There's a trap on the floor
right outside their front door.
With a nice piece of cheese,
they want it, pretty please!

They pull out their dice
to see who will risk life,
'cause if the trap springs,
loss of limb, it will bring!

Or perhaps even death,
they all hold their breath.
The lowest roll loses,
and suffers the bruises.

Young Billy the Bull
is the first mouse to roll...

His dice score a seven,
then Big Joe rolls eleven...

Here's Milton the Great,
his dice come up eight...

Next is tiny Anne Lee,
she scores only a three...

She thinks she is through,
but ol' Brick rolls a two!

Brick's done this before,
now he's at it once more.
He takes a deep sigh,
for he once lost an eye
to the trap on the floor,
that sits outside their front door.

Quickly, now quickly!
Brick must do it quickly!
Quickly, now quickly!
That is the trick, see!

Please, pretty please...
say the other mousies!
Please, pretty please...
bring us the cheese!

Flap-ity flap,
Brick runs to the trap!
Clackity-clack,
The trap goes snap!

A stinger, a stinger,
Poor Brick lost a finger!
Well...
at least the Mendenhall Mice
will have dinner.

The Pigeon
(For E.A. Poe)

'Twas a dark December
night of yore,
so long ago,
I've forgotten for sure.
But I remember a time
of lonesome looks,
as I sat reading
a bunch of old books.
Poring them over
from cover to cover,
searching for the answer
to some question or t'other.
Lumping around,
feeling sorry for my poor self,
when in flew a pigeon,
who plopped down on my shelf.

It stared with its eyes
as dull as can be,
looking hither and thither,
but not really at me.
It seemed to know something,
this solemn old bird,
so, I asked it a question,
I know that it heard.
"Is there respite
from this sorrow and pain?
Relief for this agony
that drives me insane?
Answer me, bird,
as you perch by my door.
Will I see her again,
my lost love, Lenore?
Will I be with her now
for ever and ever more?!?"

QUOTH THE PIGEON: ...

..okay, it said nothing,
and just pooped in my room.
So, I chased it away
with a dust pan and a broom.

No More Gnome

There's a gnome
in my home,
he won't leave me alone!
He grins
as he flings
all of my things!
He threw a booger
in my sugar
and ruined
my slow cooker!
He squeezed
toothpaste
in my face
and put gravy
in my Ming vase!

He jingles all his bells,
smashes my seashells,
and the worst part is
he really, really smells!
He ate the Christmas ham,
bangs the pots and pans,
and doesn't even recycle
his empty aluminum cans!
He bumps, and he jumps,
takes so many dumps!
He dances by the toilet...
Oh! he fell in!
I flushed him down with a grin...
and I hoped I'd never see
that foolish, little gnome
again!!!
                    But...

...I thought that was all,
in my bed
I did fall,
but then
I heard
those little bells
tinkling down the hall.

Closer

and closer

and closer

and closer

and closer

and closer...

...aw nuts, there he is again.

Miss me?

Frankenrocker

Thunder and lightning,
thunder and lightning!
Make the evening sky,
seem so very frightening!

Shovels and spades, hey,
shovels and spades, hey!
Goin' to the cemetery,
Gonna dig up some graves, hey!

Arms, legs, and feet, sure,
arms, legs and feet, sure!
Need to find some parts,
To build us a creature!

Don't forget the brains now,
don't forget the brains now!
Put 'em in the bag,
with the other remains now!

Piece him together, hey,
piece him together, hey!
Bind the arms and legs,
with pieces of leather, hey!

Needles and thread, yeah,
Needles and thread, yeah!
Go through the neck,
and attach it to the head, yeah!

Plug him in the wall there,
plug him in the wall there!
There's an outlet to your left,
at the end of the hall there!

See the lightning strike now,
see the lightning strike now!
Running through his body,
bring our monster to life now!

Boom, bang, slap, oh
boom, bang, slap, oh!
How I love the sound
of that big thunderclap, oh!

Here comes the shock, dude,
here comes the shock, dude!
He's starting to move,
he's starting to rock, DUDE!

But it's the strangest thing here,
it's the strangest thing here!
All he wants to do,
is hop around and sing here!

So, we gave him a guitar, yeah,
we gave him a guitar, yeah!
Now our monster is,
a heavy metal rock star... YEAH!!!

Muddy Larry

Bloody Mary!

Bloody Mary!

Bloody Mary!

Say it three times,

and you'll see something scary!

Watch her morbid image

appear in the mirror,

filling all the children

with loads and loads of fear!

But even Bloody Mary

needs to take a vacation.

So, she asks her brother Larry

to fill in for her station.

Muddy Larry!

Muddy Larry!

Muddy Larry!

Say it three times,

and it won't be very scary...

...but you'll probably have to grab
the mop and the broom,
and spend a few hours
cleaning up the bathroom!

The Problem with Spots

Lady Macbeth had a problem
with some goshdarn spots,
because they were so bloody
and covered her hands quite a lot.
She went to the drug store
and bought a bar of soap,
but did that get them out?
The answer still is nope.
She searched, and she searched,
trying all the different brands,
but there was just not a cleaner
to wash those spots from her hands.
She scrubbed, and she scoured.
Oh, how hard she tried!
But her hands, they stayed red,
until the day she died.

Pitter Patter

Pitter patter, pitter patter.
Why the long face?
What is the matter?
It's the girl in blue,
she's looking for you.
From a faraway place
with a hare and a hatter.
She fell in a hole
and lost her soul.
The Red Queen gave chase
demanding her skull on a platter.
She kept her head
but lost her mind instead.
She now spends her days
growing madder and madder.
It's the girl in blue,
she wants to play with you.
Pitter patter, pitter patter.

The Thing with So Many Eyes

The thing with so many eyes
is watching all of you guys.
No matter what you do,
no matter who you tease.
The thing with so many eyes,
it just always sees.

When Bobby went and pulled
        poor Suzy's hair.
When Scott put a tack
        on Miss Harper's chair.
When Jenny up and stole
        little Jimmy's lunch.
When Joe hit Kevin
        with a mean sucker punch.

When Ernie decided
    to ditch out on school.
When Patty called Mr. Jones
    a silly old fool.
When Lee took his Brussel sprouts
    and threw them all out.
When Lisa picked her nose
    and wiped it on mom's panty hose.
When Gerald did not think
    and went poop in the sink.
When Betty carved a 'B'
    in the old family tree.
When Carol stole some candy
    from her good friend, Mandy.
When Tom was a brat
    and pulled the tail of his cat.
The thing with so many eyes,
    it saw all of that.

So, if you've been mean,
an all around cad,
always causing a scene,
just being plain bad.

Don't be mistaken,
best say your goodbyes,
'cause you will be taken
by the thing with so many eyes.

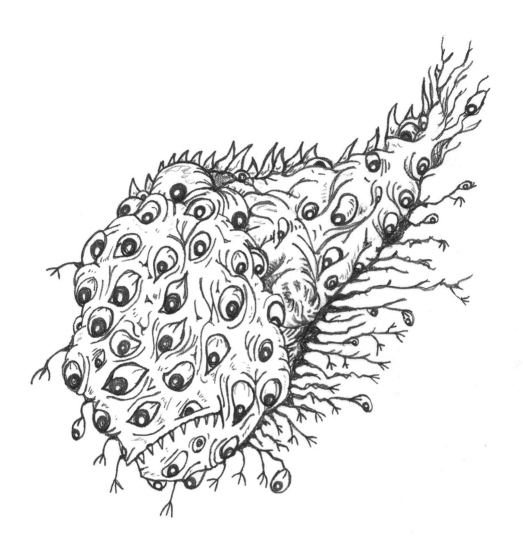

The Birthday Banshee

The birthday banshee
just wanted to sing
that special song
for every man, woman and thing!
But when she opened her mouth
and broke what was quiet,
she caused such a commotion
and nearly started a riot!
Everybody told her to stop.
They all plugged their ears,
making the poor banshee weep
such big, salty tears.
She ran far away
thinking she'd be all alone,
when another banshee called
her up on the phone.
They decided to meet,
and not be silent forever.
Now they are happy...

... SCREAMING AND SHOUTING TOGETHER!!!

Top 10 Reasons to Get out of Bed

Number 1 -
 Today will be so much fun.
Number 2 -
 I get to hang out with you.
Number 3 -
 I really have to pee.
Number 4 -
 The world outside my front door.
Number 5 -
 Potatoes with sour cream and chive.
Number 6 -
 There's a bowl of fresh Chex mix.
Number 7 -
 Game shows at eleven.
Number 8 -
 Well, life is just great!
Number 9 -
 I can do so much with my time!!
And the best reason is,
by far, Number 10

                which is...

...TONIGHT I GET
TO GO TO BED AGAIN!!!

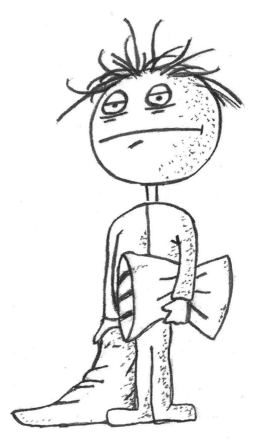

The Cranium's Conundrum

I found a skull,
it spoke to me.
I presented a question,
it answered "to be."
I thanked it kindly,
but ere I left,
the skull asked of me
one simple request.
"I have a favor,
if you don't mind,
a problem I've had
for such a long time.
You see,
I've lost my hands
since I've been dead,
making it quite hard
to scratch
this darn itch
on my head!!!"

The Old Superhero

The old superhero
looks at his cape,
filled with holes
and patched with tape.
He fought many villains
and saved many people,
helped the weak,
and protected the feeble.

He once had super strength,
and even could fly,
run really fast,
shoot laser beams with his eye.
But now he walks with a cane,
and has a bad back.
Where once there were lasers,
there are now cataracts.

He lives by himself,
and reads the paper,
sips at his coffee,
says "hello" to his neighbor.
No one remembers,
he once was the greatest,
how many times he saved the world
from being decimated.

So many bad guys,
he had kept them in line.
The only foe he cannot beat...
is the tenacious
ticking of time.

The Great Snowball Battle of Betty and the Yeti

The conditions were just right
for Betty and the yeti
to have a snowball fight.
They rolled some snow,
went toe to toe,
battling through the night.
When all was done,
neither one had won,
there was no end in sight.
This went on for weeks,
they had cold cheeks,
this war was quite a plight.
They finally agreed,
there really was no need,
their spite was not so bright.
They hugged it out,
went the peaceful route,
and Betty and the yeti
(whose name was Freddy)
enjoyed hot cocoa
under the lovely
morning light.

Large
Poems

Sir Dennis
& the Dragon

Young Dennis Quigley
awoke with a fright.
Something was wrong
in the dark, scary night.
Not sure what to do,
he stayed in his bed,
while big thoughts of terror
danced in his head.

He gripped at his blanket,
holding it so tightly.
Something was there,
something mean and unsightly.
A thick bead of sweat
formed on his brow.
He knew he must get up,
but he did not know how.

Frozen with fear,
Dennis sure could not budge.
He heard something squish,
it sounded like sludge.
Slinking and slithering,
it was under his bed.
"What could it be?"
he wondered with dread.

Dennis gathered his strength,
sitting up with a start.
But he could not keep silent,
the pounding of his poor heart.
He took a deep breath,
and counted to ten,
then leapt from his bed,
but knew not what to do then.

Standing firm to his ground,
it all seemed so quiet.
Like the calm before the storm,
or an impending riot.
His vision adjusted
to the dark of the room,
and then he heard the noise.
It sounded like doom.

Squish-Squash, Squish-Squash...
rumbled through his ears.
The sound of evil...
the sound of nightmares.
That's when he saw it,
he gasped with surprise.
Staring from under his bed,
were two big yellow eyes.

A grim and ghastly sight,
blood pupils of red.
If he did not act fast,
Dennis knew he'd be dead.
Throwing open the closet,
he saw just what he'd need...
his silly old costume
from last Halloween.

He'd gone as a knight
from King Arthur's Round Table.
A knight who was strong.
A knight who was able
to take down his foes
with a wooden broad sword,
protecting himself
with shield made from a board.

His armor from the drug store,
and made of cheap plastic,
held in place on his body
by a thin piece of elastic.
He was ready to face
any situation so grave.
No longer a boy,
now SIR DENNIS THE BRAVE!

A deep laugh now rumbled
from the thing in his room.
Echoing loudly,
like a drum that went boom.
From under his bed,
it started to creep.
The thing that woke Dennis
from his comfortable sleep.

First came the feet,
all covered with scales.
From all of the toes,
grew hideous nails.
Its legs were bright green,
and thick as tree trunks.
A belly so large,
like it had eaten three monks.

Finally, the great head
made its arrival.
Dennis gripped his sword tight,
to fight for survival.
The thing's yellow eyes
sat atop a long snout.
Horns on its head,
sharp teeth in its mouth.

A gray puff of smoke,
blew out of one nostril.
This thing seemed quite bad,
this thing seemed quite hostile.
It crushed Dennis's toys,
and kicked over his red wagon.
Sir Dennis now faced...
a huge, fire-breathing dragon!

"I am not afraid,"
Dennis shouted quite loudly.
"I have seen worse,"
he added quite proudly.
"I'll fight to the death,
to keep you at bay,
and assuming I win,
will you just go away?"

The dragon now laughed,
a deep, hearty tone.
Dennis was chilled,
chilled to the bone.
The monster opened its mouth,
Dennis thought he was a goner,
but he was quite wrong,
and could not have been
any wronger.

"I'm so tired," said the beast.
"From flying all day...
I'd like to sit for a while,
rest my feet if I may.
I've spent the last month,
searching for a small village,
to burn and to plunder,
to wreck and to pillage."

"But I have had no luck,
it's really quite unpleasant,
when one has nothing to eat,
not even a skinny peasant."
His tummy now grumbled,
this dragon looked so sad.
Dennis thought to himself,
"He really doesn't seem bad."

The dragon started to whine,
he started to moan,
"I'm so very hungry...
I'm starved to the bone!
It's a terrible thing,
for a dragon so famished,
I just want a burger,
or a nice tuna fish sandwich!"

Dennis was no longer scared,
he was in a good mood.
He could help this fellow out,
he could give him some food.
"How about some bread
with peanut butter and jelly?
That'll taste great,
that'll fill your fat belly!"

The dragon grinned brightly,
and wiped away all his tears.
"You would do that for me?
You really do care?"
"Of course, " said Dennis.
"And I'll throw in some chips."
The dragon clapped his claws,
and licked his big, juicy lips.

"Thank you so much,
you're truly a friend.
We'll be pals forever,
right up 'til the end."
Dennis laid down his sword,
there was no need to fight,
but as soon as he did,
the dragon ate him up
WITH ONE GREAT, BIG BITE!

He swallowed Dennis whole,
he belched and he sighed.
He then rubbed his tummy,
feeling quite satisfied.
He flew out the window,
his tail now waggin'.
And brave sir Dennis learned...
That's what he gets
for being nice to a dragon!

...BURP!!!

The Door
at
the End
of
the Stairs

What lies beyond the door
at the end of the stairs?
The parents won't say,
and act like they don't care.
But the children know better,
so they grow curious.
But they ask no questions,
lest the parents grow furious.

There's a lock on the door,
now why would that be?
To keep whatever's inside,
and not set it free.
They've messed with the lock,
they've tried to pick it.
Big, strong Jimmy Ross,
he even tried to kick it.

But they've had no luck,
the bolt has held tightly.
Then young Sally Anne Stevenson,
spoke up brightly.
"I have a great plan,
just wait and see...
I'll sneak into the parents' desk,
and steal the key!"

"Then we'll get in,"
she said with a wink.
"And see what's inside...
well, what do you think?"
Little Bobby Frank
did not think they should try.
So, he crouched in the corner,
and he started to cry.

The other kids laughed,
and thought he was silly.
"Don't be a baby,"
said freckle-faced Philly.
So, young Sally Anne
concocted her great plan.
Take the key in the night,
it'll be a good scam.

The children waited all day.
They sure did their best
to pass time away,
with slow games of chess.
Philly Beth won every time,
she was so darn smart.
She made checking your king
seem like a great art.

Next came checkers,
when other games had grown old.
"I will beat you all!"
said Jimmy Ross who was bold.
But to win any games,
he just was not able.
So, he got really mad,
and flipped over the table.

By this time it was dark,
and night filled the air,
with cold, deathly silence,
all children beware.
They soon became quiet,
and made not a sound.
The parents slept tightly,
no adults were around.

Bobby Frank hoped the others,
would all change their minds.
Just forget this plan,
leave the doorway behind.
The moment was now,
would they stick to it?
The door seemed to say,
"Go ahead, just do it."

Sally Anne snuck into the desk,
and opened the drawer,
filled with paper and pencils,
hard candy and more.
She searched for the key,
oh, where could it be???
Finally she found it,
her heart filled with glee!

A paper stuck to its end,
Sally took it and read,
"Never, ever use this key..."
is what the note said.
Sally crumbled up the paper,
and threw it on the floor.
"I'm going to use this key
to open up that door."

She returned to the children,
quiet as death,
"Please put it back,"
Bobby said under his breath.
They paid him no heed,
and went about their own way.
These children were foolish,
thinking this was okay.

Making short work of the steps,
they took them in pairs.
Soon they had reached,
the door at the end of the stairs.
Pausing for a second,
then counting to three,
Sally Anne found the lock,
and shoved in the key.

It turned with a snap,
it turned with a click.
One more turn of the key,
that would now do the trick.
Sally heard the bolt pop,
she heard the door creak.
The children all gathered 'round,
to have themselves a peek.

Except for young Bobby,
who took a step back.
He was sore afraid,
this felt like a trap.
"Please close the door,"
he begged one more time.
The others all ignored him,
and opened the door wide.

Sally Anne, she went first,
even though Bobby did warn her.
It was all very still, except...
something lurked in the corner.
"Bring in a flashlight,"
Sally Anne now called back.
But Jimmy and Philly,
had not thought about that.

They had already entered,
and were about to turn 'round,
when a scratch on the wall
made a horrible sound.
A shadow started to move,
it looked not like a man,
Jimmy started to shiver,
something cold touched his hand.

They could not see in the dark,
but they felt in their bones.
They were not by themselves,
they were by no means alone.
Sally took a step back,
the floor slick and slimy.
She froze in her tracks,
"there's something behind me..."

The door, it slammed shut,
and trapped them inside.
Sally, Jimmy and Philly,
were now quite terrified.
They tried to fight,
they tried to run,
but no matter what they did,
this could not be undone.

Falling and crying,
they rushed the door in a pack,
but something kept reaching
and pulling them back.
Trying to scream,
trying to shout...
They were stuck behind the door,
without a way out.

In the safe, quiet hall,
Bobby Frank had stayed clear.
When he saw the door shut,
he took a step near.
All was silent and still,
Bobby trembled with fear.
His friends now locked behind,
the door at the end of the stairs.

Bobby waited all night,
until the parents awoke.
He told them what happened,
and tried not to choke.
"They went into the room,"
he sputtered and spat.
"The door closed behind them...
and they never came back!"

"Who went into the room?"
the parents all did demand.
Bobby then told them
"Jimmy and Philly and, of course,
                              Sally Anne."

The parents just frowned
and looked at each other.
They sipped on their coffee
and muttered, "oh, brother."

They opened the door,
now it was clear.
The parents looked in,
"there's nothing in there."
Bobby was shocked,
past the door he now ran.
"What has happened to
Jimmy and Philly and, of course,
                              Sally Anne?"

The parents all sighed,
finally one of them spoke.
"We don't know any of those people...
is this some kind of joke?"

"They were my friends,
staying here for the night,"
young Bobby Frank said,
pleading his plight.

But the parents just stared,
and rubbed at their chins.
Scratching on their heads,
they said once again,
"We don't know any person,
child, woman or man,
named Jimmy or Philly or, of course,
Sally Anne.

Bobby remembered a picture,
sitting on his nightstand.
A photo of him and his friends,
when they all played in band.
He ran to his room,
swiped the pic off the shelf.
But when he looked at it now,
he was all by himself.

Jimmy Ross and his tuba
were no longer there.
Philly Beth and her drum
had both disappeared.
Sally Anne and her trumpet,
gone to some place unknown.
In that picture on his shelf,
Bobby now stood alone.

"Come have some breakfast,"
the parents insisted.
It was as if the others,
simply never existed.
Bobby Frank nibbled some bacon,
and shed a few tears.
He knew
        his friends
                had been
                        taken...

...by the door
        at
          the end
              of
                the stairs.

Christmas with the Tiniest Vampire

The tiniest vampire
lived in an old shoe.
Where he came from,
nobody knew.
A corner of the room
is where he staked claim.
In an old shoe
with somebody's name.

Chuck Taylor it read,
on the side of the sneaker.
The tiny vampire thought,
"that name is a keeper."
So, he called himself 'Chuck',
Mr. Taylor to you.
For his real name, you see,
he just never knew.

The tiny vampire's life,
to himself was a mystery.
He knew naught of his birth
nor family history.
But he didn't mind,
so long as he had a cold bed.
This shoe would be fine,
now he'd sleep like the dead.

He curled up tightly,
this little fella named Chuck.
He'd snore through the winter,
if he had any luck.
Nothing would disturb him,
he truly did believe.
But he was quite wrong,
for it was Christmas Eve.

He'd hardly a wink,
when there arose such a clatter.
He sprang from his shoe
to see what was the matter.
Stumbling across the floor,
he tripped over a match,
tore his cape on a nail
that it happened to catch.

The vampire grew grumpy,
his mind was now seething.
Who had made this noise
that kept him from sleeping?
He collected his thoughts,
to this person he'd say,
"I'm trying to sleep,
will you please go away?"

Up to the window,
he flew like a flash,
tore open the shutters,
and threw up the sash.
When, what to his bloodshot
yellow eyes should appear?
But a miniature sleigh
and eight tiny reindeer.

With a lively old driver,
so plump and so thick,
he knew in a moment,
it must be St. Nick.
The tiny vampire smiled,
he could not believe his eyes.
This would be such a treat,
this Christmas surprise.

His eyes turned a bright red,
as he licked at his fangs.
His tummy now growled
with great hunger pangs.
"Soon, I'll be fine," he thought
as he drooled.
"After I suck all the blood
from this fat, jolly fool."

And then in a twinkling,
he heard on the roof,
the prancing and pawing
of each little hoof.
The vampire hid in a corner
and did not make a sound.
Down the chimney, old Santa
came with a bound.

His eyes, how they twinkled,
his dimples so merry!
His cheeks were like roses,
his blood like a cherry!
He had a broad face
and a gruesome, round belly
that shook when he walked,
like a barrel full of jelly.

"I'll take him now,"
the vampire did think.
He was ready to eat,
he was ready to drink!
He sprang from the corner,
preparing to strike,
hissing as loud as he could,
to fill his victim with fright.

But St. Nick did not scream,
nor did he shout.
He just smiled and asked,
"what's this fuss all about?"
The tiny vampire was shocked,
he knew not what to say.
"I'm gonna suck your blood,"
he mumbled...
"Then call it a day."

"Oh-ho-ho-ho,"
Santa just laughed,
and jiggled his gut,
"Let's make a deal..."
he grinned...
"Here, I'll tell ya what."

"I have something in my bag,
something for you...
something so big and so bright...
something shiny and new."

"A gift for me?"
The vampire found
believing this hard.
For he had never
received a gift.
Not even a card.

"Yes, something for you!
Now, what's your name, sailor?"
The vampire looked at the floor,
and quietly said...
"Chuck Taylor."

"Oh-ho-ho-ho!"
Santa boomed, and he grinned.
He reached in his bag,
"I have just the thing!"

The tiny vampire wondered,
"What could it be?
Something full of blood,
something waiting for me?
To sink in my teeth,
and suck it quite dry,
a cricket or a grasshopper...
or a plump, juicy fly!!!
Oh, I can't wait!
This is so very exciting!
Even a fat roach...
would be so inviting!!!"

Santa spoke not a word,
but went straight to work.
He reached into his bag,
before turning like a jerk.
His eyes twinkled with glee,
his teeth shone like a beaker.
He held out the gift...
a brand new all-star
basketball sneaker!

The vampire was shocked,
this was not what he expected.
His dream of plump, juicy flies,
suddenly Santa had wrecked it.
The fat fool laughed
and threw his hands on his hips.
He jiggled and bounced,
while the vampire
now pursed his lips.

169.

"Oh-ho-ho-ho,"
Santa laughed
like a nut case.
He leaned down close,
and got in
the tiny vampire's face.

"Well, what do you think?
Do you love my
gift just for you?"

The vampire smirked,
and he said...
"I already have a shoe."

With a blink of his eye,
and a twist of his head,
Santa soon knew,
he had something to dread.

We'll stop right here...
keep the story
covered in fog.
Let's just say...
the vampire drank too much
that night...
and it wasn't egg nog.

But before he was finished
with this unpleasant sight,
the tiny vampire called out,
"scary Christmas to all...
and to all a good fright!!!"

SAFE

Something is amiss
in the dark, scary night.

The creatures are unable
to scare up a fright!

The monster
under your bed
is taking a snooze.

The ghosts
in the corner
are singing the blues!

The boogeyman
is killing time
checking his email.

Lol.

The werewolf
is busy
chasing his own tail.

The demons
are playing
silly games
on their phones.

The skeletons
are laughing
at their own
funny bones.

The zombie
is struggling
to write
a love letter.

Brains are red,
brains are blue,
how I wish
I could eat
your brains, too.

Bloody Mary
is knitting
a nice
Christmas sweater.

The tentacle beast
is eating
peanut butter
and s'mores.

The creepy clown
went shopping
at the ol'
grocery store.

The vampires
are judging
each other's
new looks.

This is a
good one.

So is this one.

And this one!

And the thing with
so many eyes
is reading
so many books!

The monsters
in your room
must find something
else to do.

Because they
haven't got
the power
to frighten you.

Fiddlesticks.

They certainly would,
if they had
their druthers.

But lucky
for you,
you're safe...

... under the covers.

I'd like to unravel a
gigantic
round of applause
for the
Tiniest Vampire Fan Club!!!

Aaron & Juli Hendren, Adeline Lilly Francis,
Alisha Ray, Alistair, Amitai Cohen
Amy Bourque, Anastasia Thompson,
Andi Januskiewicz, Andrew Elliott,
Andy & Joan, Angelica C. Bernstein,
Anne Haney, Anne Mewburn-Gray,
Asa Crowe, Ashley, Ashley Brown,
Audrey Wallander, Ava Mandeville,
Beatrix Aurit, Ben B., Benjamin Nichols,
Blue, Bobby Ghaheri, Brian & Kay Cunnane,
Brian & Lizzie Wenrich, Bridget S. Dunne,
Bruce Wong, Caleb Herring, Carissa Mitchell,
Carys Mathews, Casey Mraz, Cat Homlish,
Chan Ka Chun Patrick,
Charlie William Murphy Wheeler,
Charlotte Boo Chew, Charlotte Hillery,
Christina Cavaleri, Christine Chang,
Christy Lopez, Christopher James Sidebottom,
Chris Suski & Sarah Katz Suski,
Cindy Gonzales, Claudio MeoPeo
Connor Spurlock, Courtney Bradbury,
Craig A. Butler, Craig Anderson, Cris Swenson,
Cyndi Trissel, Dale Wick, Dani Adams,

Daniel T. Cornish & Tiffani E. Cornish,
Daniel Runde, Daniella Yasmin Sayer,
Darci Fredricks, Darcie Farrow,
Davey Rogulich, David Tipping, David Valdez,
Dawn Briggs, Debi, Denise Schulz,
Derek E. Ladd, Devin O'Leary, Doug Montoya,
Drew Morrison, Duncan Monié, Eddie Dean,
Elena Lara Lucia Nuno Figueiredo Batão,
Elizabeth Henning, Ellie Lawson,
Elliot Jackson, Emma Kimbell, Erin Damm,
Erin K. MOOTS, Ethan Glenn-Reller,
Eugene & Carrie Adams,
Eugene Loo, Evonne Okafor, Fairlie Giles,
Felicia & The Doc, Fenja Solveig Schadagies,
Gabrielle Aimee, George Bach,
Glenn Pa Moore, Gregory Wong, Hayden G.,
Heather Blackhurst, Heather Maru,
Henry Owen Vagi, Hillery Koontz,
Hudson Hughes, Hugo Gabriel Duff, J,
Jack, Asher and Rhys Levy, James Kwan,
Jamie Jenkins, Jamie Vigliotti,
Jason & Starla Barrett,
Jeff Zwirek, Jeffrey Weiss, Jen Stephenson,

Jeri Surls, Jess Jones, Jess Selbee-Satterfield
Jessica Goodwin, Jessica Petriello,
Joanna Furgal, Jocelyn Ortez & David Mappes,
John Orr, Jose Castro, JrJr, Judith Segal,
karyngene, Kate & Peter, Kate Schroeder,
Kathleen Miller, Kathryn Kramer, Kati Bowlin,
Katie Farmin, Katy Houska, Katy Rice,
Ken Whelan, Kenna Harris, Kiah Fowler,
Kim Weithman, Kimberly Golden,
Kristin Berg, Kristin Hansen,
Kristy & Kaden Corey, Lance Arthur Smith,
Laura Kosky, Laura Rooney, Lauren Poole,
LbiGirl Beach, Lee Francis, Leigh Hile,
Leonard & Jane Witter, Leon Christopher,
Leslie Nesbit, Leslie Rachel Krafft, Lisa,
Liz Hereford, Lupe H. Preciado, Lydia Au,
M. Rebecca Nadler, MaccaBot,
Maddox & Ronan, Madelaine Simons,
Marcela Perez, Maren Parriott, Maria Friesen,
Marisa Sleeter, Marita Meegan,
Mark & Sonja Carey,
Mark Chavez, Marnie Henke,
Martin Eichelmann, Martin Gooch,

Mat Masding-Grouse, Matt & Mandy Nixon,
Matt Heath, Matthew Lawrence Urbaniak,
Mauricio Abril, Megan CW, Mel Phey,
Micah Linford, Michael Alazard,
Michael Newlyn Blake, Michael Wallace,
Michael Wolthusen, Mike "Call Me
Superman" Wilson, Mike Johnson,
Miranda de Quadros, Monika Mackowiak,
Morgan & Tiffany Witter, Mrittika Ghosh,
Mulcuto Razors, Naomi Hazuki Boat,
Natasha Ali, Nathan "They" Williams,
Nick Ganjei, Nicole Duke, Nicole Gillig,
Nicole Lopez, Nicole Wilkinson, Nina Cottrell,
Nova Clarke, Olive Barrett,
Patricia Jensen, Paul Rozand, Peter Kierst
Phillip Hughes & Jennifer Daugherty,
Piero Arba, Pumpkin, Rachel Hroncich,
Radha Denmark, Ray & Beth Welt,
Reynalden Delgarito, Richard Stovall,
Ridley & Riley Censon, Rik, Rob Buco,
Robert Zhang, Roisin McCormac, Ross Kelly,
Ryan Coffman, Ryan Denmark, Ryan Moore,
S.K., Sam Staggs, Samantha J. Shuma,

Samantha Montgomery, Sarah, Sarah Mowrey,
Scott Bryan, Scott Phillips, Sean Dowling,
Sean Motyl, Shenoah Allen, Sierra Cherniak,
Simon Platt, Stafford Douglas,
Stefan Einarson, Steve & Heather Yeocero,
Suguru Oikawa, Teagan Gacuk,
The Other Pit Man, Tim & Audrey Kirk,
Timothy Kordic, Tina Benjamin,
Tommy & Miranda, Tristan Hulse, Tyler Kent,
Vannah, Viktor & Aleksander,
Violet Knightly, Virginia Ludvik,
Wendy Scott, Winston Kou, Yvette Givens,
Zack Newman, Zöe Alexandra Hayman

THANK YOU!!!!!!

Jason L. Witter received his
MFA in Theatre
from the University of New Mexico.
Some of his other works include:
"Cap'n Hook" and "Mimi and the Ghosts" -
plays for young audiences
&
"The Things That Live in Your House" -
a horror rhyme for the inquisitive mind

witterworks1@gmail.com

www.facebook.com/witterworks

Made in the USA
Charleston, SC
14 March 2016